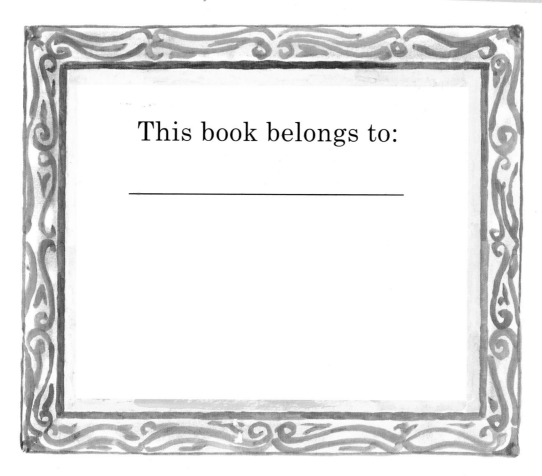

This book belongs to:

_____

For Madeline and Luca

Matthew's Dream

Leo Lionni

ANDERSEN PRESS

A couple of mice lived in a dusty attic with their only child. His name was Matthew. In one corner of the attic, draped with cobwebs, were piles of newspapers, books and magazines, an old broken lamp and the sad remains of a doll.

That was Matthew's corner.

The mice were very poor, but they had high hopes for Matthew.
He would grow up to be a doctor, perhaps.
Then they would have Parmesan cheese for breakfast, lunch and dinner.
But when they asked Matthew what he wanted to be, he said,
"I don't know . . .
I want to see the world."

One day Matthew and his classmates were
taken to the museum.
It was the first time.

They were amazed at what they saw.
There was a huge portrait of King Mouse the Fourth, dressed like a general.
And next to it was a picture of cheese that made Matthew drool.
There were winged mice that floated through the air and mice with horns and bushy tails.
And mountains and rushing streams and branches bowing in the wind. The world is all here, thought Matthew.

Entranced, Matthew wandered from room to room
gazing at the paintings. There were some that he
didn't understand at first.
One looked like crusts of pastry, but when he
looked more carefully, a mouse emerged.

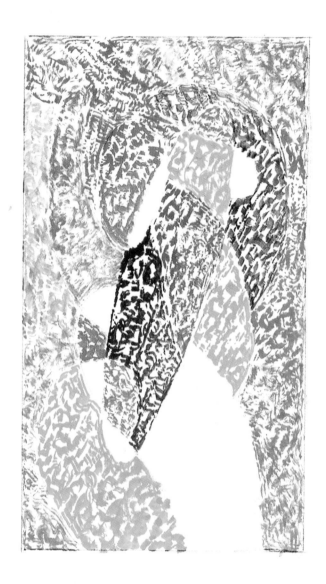

Then, turning the corner, Matthew found himself
face to face with another little mouse.
She smiled at him. "I am Nicoletta," she said.
"Aren't these paintings wonderful?"

That night Matthew had a strange dream.
He dreamed that he and Nicoletta
were walking, hand in hand, in an immense,
fantastic painting.

As they walked, playful patches of colour shifted under their feet and all around them suns and moons moved gently to the sound of distant music.

Matthew had never been so happy. He embraced Nicoletta. "Let's stay here forever," he whispered.

Matthew woke with a start. He was alone.
Nicoletta had faded with his dream.
The grey dreariness of his attic corner appeared
to him in all its bleak misery.
Tears came to his eyes.

But then, as if by magic, what Matthew saw began to change.
The shapes hugged each other and the pale colours of the
messy junk heap brightened.
Even the crumpled newspapers now looked soft and smooth.
And from afar Matthew thought he heard the notes of a
familiar music.

He ran to his parents' corner.
"I know!" he said. "Now I know!
I want to be a painter!"

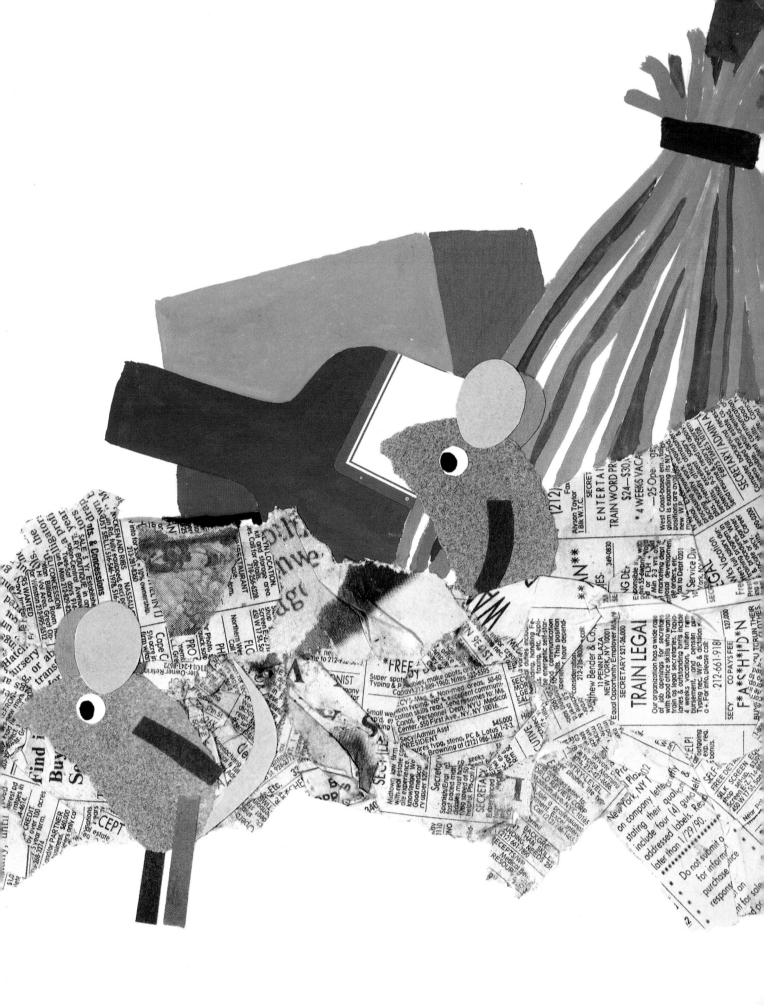

Matthew became a painter.
He worked hard and painted large canvases
filled with the shapes and colours of joy.

Then he married Nicoletta.
In time he became famous, and mice
from all over the world came to see
and buy his paintings.

His largest painting now
hangs in the museum.
When asked about the title,
Matthew smiles.
"The title?" he says as if he
had never thought about
it before.
"My dream."

Also by Leo Lionni:

9781849393096

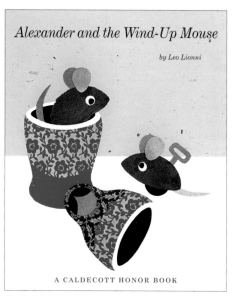

9781849397056

This paperback edition first published in 2014 by Andersen Press Ltd.
First published in Great Britain in 2014 by Andersen Press Ltd.,
20 Vauxhall Bridge Road, London SW1V 2SA.
Published in Australia by Random House Australia Pty.,
Level 3, 100 Pacific Highway, North Sydney, NSW 2060.
Originally published in hardcover in the United States by Pantheon Books,
A division of Random House, LLC., New York, in 1991.
Copyright © 1991 by Leo Lionni.
Published by arrangement with Random House Children's Books,
a division of Random House, LLC, New York, New York, U.S.A.
All rights reserved.
Printed and bound in Singapore by Tien Wah Press.
10 9 8 7 6 5 4 3 2 1
British Library Cataloguing in Publication Data available.
ISBN 978 1 78344 056 6